Selina Dorado

Mes Amours

Poems: Passionate and Playful

Selina Dorado

Mes Amours
Poems: Passionate and Playful

ISBN/EAN: 9783744711791

Printed in Europe, USA, Canada, Australia, Japan

Cover: Foto ©Andreas Hilbeck / pixelio.de

More available books at **www.hansebooks.com**

"MES AMOURS:"

Poems: Passionate and Playful

WRITTEN TO ME BY PEOPLE CELEBRATED AND OBSCURE
AND
MY ANSWERS TO SOME OF THEM

WITH AN INTRODUCTION AND NOTES.

———

SELINA DOLARO

L'Amour est enfant de Bohème !
—CARMEN.

————

CHICAGO AND NEW YORK
BELFORD, CLARKE & COMPANY
1888

PREFATORY EXCURSION BY WAY OF EX-PLANATION AND APOLOGY.

DURING the happy years that I acted as the servant of a public that appreciated my efforts in that direction, I was a continual target for the metrical effusions of people—known and unknown—who sought by this means to make the acquaintance of that mysterious thing, "a popular actress;" and I frequently preserved them. On receipt of these verses I often felt myself in a position to criticise them, and even to correct their errors of orthography, syntax, metre, rhyme, and rhythm ; and, as a not unnatural result, I woke one day like Hafiz, the Persian dreamer, "stringing pearls of verse." The rhymes I received and the rhymes I wrote, I have at length determined to collect and publish.

It may be that I render myself liable to criticism in acceding to the requests which have been made me to publish these verses and sketches—caricatures literary and artistic, I might say—that have been sent me from time to time. But as circumstances are always allowed to alter cases, I claim "circumstances" (in fact, with a certain political faction, I "claim everything"). Few persons are privileged to read their virtues, abilities, and attractions extolled in ante- [by way of post-] mortem notices, written in anticipation of immediate dissolution. Such was my fate. For the first time I learned that I was clever and beautiful. Dangerous things to tell a woman ! True, I was expected to take my leave of this mundane sphere respectably, pathetically, and, above all, immediately. It really was my duty to have done so. I must admit a want of tact on this occasion. I have, as a rule, a keen sense of the fitness of things, but the fitness of this particular thing was altogether *too* fit ; and, in spite of the very pretty funeral mine would have been (for it was not long since I had appeared on the stage looking very young and—etc., as above), I behaved most inconsiderately, and continued to live. Henceforth I became a curiosity, and poor mankind became my victim. There is a charming uncertainty as to when my picturesque end will come—a delightful expectancy of my final *coup de théâtre*—that affords me immunity from all rules. These are my "circumstances." So much by way of explanation.

I have always been a trial to my friends, but this last departure of mine is, I am bound to admit, cruel. That I should write a play was bad, very bad—my only excuse was that I knew something of the stage ; but to scatter doggerel in my wake (not in the Hibernian sense) is still worse. I can offer no valid reason for, no palliation of, my offence. However, the sooner I am cured the better ; and what better cure could I find than the gentle (I am sure) but determined "sitting-on" I shall get for my temerity ? From my poor friends I ask forgiveness. To my enemies I dedicate that portion of this volume which comes from my pen, as a sufficient retribution.

In the notes I have endeavoured to record truthfully my impressions on receiving said verses, and the feelings that prompted me to retort in doggerel of my own. It is unnecessary for me to say that I think the former are good and the latter bad. Anyone can say that.

SELINA DOLARO.

NEW YORK, November, 1887.

CONTENTS.

OTHER PEOPLE'S.

MY OWN.

OTHER PEOPLE'S.

MA BELLE AMIE.

NOTE.—One of the few *genuine* poems that have been sent me, expressing, as it does, the feelings of a thoroughly *lazy* adorer. He resembles the degenerate ones in "The Water Babies," who refused to take the trouble to chase the roasted pig, or climb the trees whereon the flap-doodle grew.

I.

I do not love you in the least,

This is a poetical form of the words "without prejudice," that a lawyer puts on his letters when he's afraid to compromise himself.

Ma belle amie ;
That sentiment long since has ceased,
Ma belle amie.
And yet there's something near my heart
That hurts a little when we part ;
'Tis sweet, and yet it leaves a smart,

Simile: The Christmas cracker.

Ma belle amie !

II.

Your cheek is soft, and fair to see,

My sentiments exactly, on reading the first verse.

Ma belle amie ;
Your lips are sweet—too sweet for me,
Ma belle amie.
I long, and yet I fear to press
That bosom in my wild caress,
Lest I should love you more—or less,

This circumspection is the philosophy of bards.

Ma belle amie !

III.

Since Friendship seems a trifle cold,
This should have been headed "The Lay of the Lazy Lover."
                Ma belle amie;
And Love, you say, would be too bold,
                Ma belle amie;
We'll split the diff'rence 'twixt the two,
And feel—just as the Angels do :
That is—I hardly know—do you ?
                Ma belle amie!

AFTER-THOUGHT.—Very charming and non-committal, like the trousers purchased by a frugal mamma for her eldest boy, with a view to the "wrong side" for purposes of turning and altering for the youngest.

COSTI
FAN
TUTTI

A QUESTION.

NOTE.—A poem written by a bard who caused himself to be presented to me after the per-
formance of " La Perichole." One of the few copies of verse that show internal evidence of
having been written for me alone. A very insidious form of poem, as it leaves one complete
liberty of action—a liberty that one is bound to misuse.

WAS it a chance—or Providence—or what
    That, on that fateful night,
Led my vague footsteps to the magic spot
    That *you* filled in with light?

> Why do bards ask these sort of questions? Is it because they scan
> easily, or is it the natural and irresponsible curiosity of bards?

Was it a chance—mere waywardness of yours—
    That caused your smile to say
That I was different to the gaping boors

> Was there ever a man who didn't think this?

    Who came to see your play?

> Good! This assumption is good, because by giving one the chance
> to tell the bard he is mistaken, he prompts one to say he is right,
> and thank him for saving one trouble.

At least I read that message in them then;
    And, though I laughed to think
That I—the worst-used, bitterest of men—
    Should find another brink

Of love to tremble on, yet in my heart
  I knew the laugh untrue :
I saw the actress play the soulless part,
  But through her I saw *you.*

> Very delicate and insinuating, and all the more charming as I don't
> think any other woman ever had *this* particular poem.

Behind *La Perichole* I knew there lived
  A woman—"nobly planned"—
Oh! that grand night, when I so well contrived
  To touch your little hand!

> It *was* clever. If I remember rightly, he was presented, [I think, out
> of spite,] by a man who hated him. A grand "send-off" for a
> man, if he only knew.

And you?   Were "profits" in your mind just then,
  Or was it but—caprice?
Was I an unit 'mongst the amorous men
  Who came to see your piece?

> The bard is mistaken.   I had no financial interest in the play.

Or was it different?   Before 'tis o'er—
  Our little dream of love—

> "Dream" is good, but "my" would have been better.

And I must pass outside your jealous door,
  And know you sit above,

> Bless me! does he mean when I am dead?

Forgetting me—on purpose—putting me
  Out of your life as vain—

> Apparently not. Thanks!

Tell me the truth, my Dolly—can it be
That I was loved again ?

What a question ! And from a man, too, who knew his Balzac by
heart !

AFTER-THOUGHT.—Prettily composed, but rather an unwise poem to send. Not suffi-
ciently proprietary and deprecating—two qualities that ought always to "jump to the eyes"
concomitantly in an amateur love-effusion. Still, as I said in the NOTE, this gives one a dangerous latitude of action.

A MEMORY.

[AFTER DOLLY HAD CALLED UPON ME.]

NOTE.—A clever poem, because it unites within itself three magic qualities : First, it is of the adaptable kind, and may be sent to anyone on account of its impersonality ; second, it expresses a state of rabid adoration without calling for any responsive effort on one's own part ; and third, it is a purely *ex-parte* statement (to speak legally), and does not pretend to assume that one in any way reciprocates the delirium one has produced.

A PERFUMED delirium steals thro' the air,
 As I sit here alone, and the fire-light dies ;
And you stand here again, with your exquisite hair,
    Quite right not to compromise himself on color.
 With your passionate lips and your pleading eyes.

It was here that you sat—if I stretch out my hand
 I can almost believe that I touch you again ;
Like the hunger-mad sailor who springs for the land
 That he sees in his madness—but springs for in vain.
    Expressive, this !

Do mad people *know* they are mad—do you think ?
 And do the dead *know* they are dead ?—tell me this :
I care not ! for I should be willing to sink
 Into madness or death 'neath the spell of your kiss.
   I wonder——well, never mind, I think I'll let this verse go as it is.

You're here once again—leaning back in this chair,
And I am content to crouch here at your knee ;
In the flesh you are distant—but what do I care
That your body is there, since your soul is with me.

A most convenient lover—would that there were more like unto him !

I hold you still closer—your breath on my cheek
Drives the blood through my veins like a torrent of flame,
Whilst *I* dare not breathe. If my soul could but speak,
The Echoes Eternal would answer *your* name.

Again very cleverly uncompromittal ! A very cautious bard. A swain
once shouted my name at an echo, and it answered nothing but
" Jolly " and " Folly."

And now ? It is morning—you're still in my grasp,
As I shut close my door ; and I put out my light,
And I lie here. Alone ? Do you think I unclasp
My arms from your neck ?—do I bid you "Good-night ?"
Ah, no !

AFTER-THOUGHT.—If all bards had the imagination, and resources within themselves for self-
delusion, that this one had, *nous autres femmes* would lead a much pleasanter and *mâle* existence. The one dreadful danger of the above is that its luridity and sultriness, and yet perfect
contentment, tempt one to " make an experience," saying, " That's all very well, but *if*—etc.,
etc."

2

YOUR BIRTHDAY.

NOTE.—A patent title; like all the finest patents, valuable on account of its supreme simplicity —a title that covers a multitude of sins. This poem, however, is designed for sending when the "*affaire*" is in full swing, and has a taste of spurious eternity; very pleasant, even when one has "been there before," so to speak.

I.

YOUR birthday! To think you were living
  For years before now: it is queer,
For I—to my friends—have been giving
  The date of my birth as *this* year;

> An antique sentiment, but always pleasant. The only man who ever said it truthfully was Adam.

And yet I am older than you!

> *Vide suprà*, concerning Adam.

My theory's right, and it's pleasant;
  Put by that old bogey, the Past:
We only are made for the Present,
  To live while each new love can last.

> Verse warranted to kill in the earlier stages, when one is afraid of being bored.

We're not a year old, dear, we two!

II.

We were born, when your soft hand in mine, dear,
  Was clasped on that glorious day;
When we vowed that our lives must combine, dear,
  Whatever the world might say—

> [And what is the world when you woo?]

> Deadly irresponsibility apparently, but quite harmless in the majority of cases.

We shall live while our hearts beat together,
  A summer of flow'ry delight ;
And what need we care for the weather,
  When all in our hearts is so bright ?
      Our sunshine is there, sweet, in *you !*

Very previsional ; leaves independence of action in reserving the right
to say, some-day, " *You* put the light out."

III.

If the life we are only beginning,
  With the love that has caused it, should fail ;
There are lovers more worthy the winning,
  So why should my darling bewail ?

Irresponsible humility ; very reassuring when one isn't quite sure of
one's self.

      The Present is sweet and is *true !*
Away with the Future ! Its pages
May turn by themselves : you and I
By kisses alone mark the ages—
  Too happy to think or to die.
      We're not a year old, dear, we two !

AFTER-THOUGHT.—A master-piece of preliminary poetry. Can only be written, however,
before you have had "scenes." Resembles, in many respects, the full blaze of a theatre-chan-
delier, which outshines the tiny, everlasting flame that lights all the others when the gas is turned
on, but goes on burning when *la grande flamme* is dead.

YOUR BIRTHDAY.

NOTE.—A great rarity, and therefore presented almost without comment. A *genuine* poem, which means what it says—the kind of verses one believes in, if one wants to.

ANOTHER year begun !   It seems
   So strange to think that you and I
Must be together but in dreams,
   Until the months have wearied by.

We have some mem'ries that are sweet :
   And in my dreams I see again
Those loving eyes, those lips I meet
   In kisses that are almost pain.

For—in them—all my heart goes out
   To meet the heart that beats for me.
Oh, darling ! I begin to doubt
   If I can bear my misery.

I want you !   All the world is cold,
   And at your heart I fain would rest ;
My cares are hung'ring to be told ;
   My head, to pillow on your breast.

Was there a time—it scarce can be—
 When you and I had never met ;
Had never let the minutes flee,
 And found it glory to forget.

Your birthday ! Let the years go past—
 Our love, my sweet, is young and strong ;
And *when* we meet to break our fast,
 Our feast of kisses shall be long.

That shall your birthday be ! *This* year
 We will expunge with all disdain :
When next I kiss away your tear,
 Then, darling, we will live again.

AFTER-THOUGHT.—He meant it.

TO MĀHMOURÉ ON HER BIRTHDAY.

MY DEAR MĀHMOURÉ :

What day has more worth
Than *this* of all others, the day of your birth?

Ah ! would that in language both witty and terse
I could honour th'occasion in apposite verse.

How strangely propitious the skies must have been,
At the moment you made your *début* on *this* scene—
On that day when each 'osophy, 'mancy, and 'ology
"Took a back seat," giving place to Astrology.

For surely your charms must be mainly dependant
On Planets that happened to be "in ascendant,"
When most of them said, "We regret that between us
We ne'er *can* produce such perfection as Venus :
For none of us *can* give our children such graces,
Such movements, such manners, such figures, such faces ;

Tho' the world may admire *our* work when 'tis done,
'Tis the children of Venus who have 'all the fun.'"

True, *I* was not there, so I cannot remember
What stars "ruled" the sky 'twixt July and September;

> Good ! August *is* a difficult word to find a rhyme to.

But surely that sky must have been wondrous bright,
With planets propitious that day—or that night.

How do I know?   Kindly pause to reflect
That I've e'er been a student of "cause and effect ;"

> This is enough to make Dugald Stewart turn in his grave, and turn
> Herbert Spencer's hair white, were it not that he has hardly any
> and what he has is already white !

And the happiest hours I've known—this is *true*—
Have been spent by the side, dear Māhmouré, of *you*.

AFTER-THOUGHT.—I wonder if this is a patent-adaptable one. It sounds like it. There is
a dangerous impersonality about it, which is not conducive to implicit confidence in its "unique-
ness."

ON THE SUN-BLACKENED PROOF OF A PHOTO, FOUND IN A NOVEL LENT ME BY DOLLY.

NOTE.—Nothing like a photo to inspire verse—one can take one's time over it. If one sits and gazes at a thing long enough, one becomes fascinated—psychological fact, not claimed as original. A proof obliterated by exposure to the light is treasure-trove to an adorer—the "flotsam, jetsam, and walend" of love; though he knows it is one's own, it makes a great opportunity for a *scène de jalousie*.

You lent me a favourite book, Dolly,
  Yestre'en, when you bade me "Good-night!"
Ere you lend one a book, you should look, Dolly,
  To see that that book is "all right."

    This is the one valuable point contained in this poem. *Experto crede,*
    as the Latin grammar says.

You hadn't touched this for an age, Dolly—
  For five years at least, perhaps more—
And turning a page—to my rage—Dolly,
  A photo dropped out on the floor!
And I sat and I glared at that thing, Dolly,
  And thought, "Whose the deuce can it be?"

    So do I. I haven't an idea.

When I show you that thing, will it bring, Dolly,
  Recollections that are *not* of me?

    Probably.

I "snorted," in picking it up, Dolly
  ['Twas red, and I felt like a bull];
But I frankly confess that my cup, Dolly,
  Of mortification was full,

And I wished that I'd let it lie there, Dolly ;
  'Twas *not* a sensation of fun,
When I found nothing there, foul or fair, Dolly—
  'Twas a proof that had been in the sun !
How wondrous are the works of Providence !

Perhaps it bore your pretty face, Dolly,
  Or that of Lord A—— or young B——?
Perhaps.

Would that I could efface ev'ry trace, Dolly,
  Of that image, that wasn't of *me ;*
But the sun had completed his task, Dolly—
  There wasn't a line to be seen.
Vide supra, concerning Providence.

I only can ask, "'Neath this mask, Dolly,
  What face—years ago—might have been ?"
I should like to imagine 'twas *yours,* Dolly ;
  But ah ! I can hardly believe
That of photo of yours—you have scores, Dolly,
  A proof in your " pet book " you'd leave.
The author was a person of keen perceptive faculties.

There isn't much doubt in my mind, Dolly,
  That here was the face of some swain
To whom you were kind—which you'll find, Dolly,
  Not hard to call up once again.
This is an error.

And you'll *not* hold this knowledge aloof, Dolly,
  When I ask when *this* love you forsook ;
Had you fled from his roof, when this proof, Dolly,
  You kept and preserved in *his* book ?
Haven't the slightest idea. I fancy he hadn't a roof !

Dolly's Answer.

Lord bless you ! 'twas a photograph of me—no doubt a
  fright—
Of which I only had the proof, and left it in the light ;

I sat for it, no doubt, one day, entirely forgetting
That " All pictures must be paid for [horrid rule] at time of
    *set*ting."

      . [*So the finished photos never came home, and I stuck that
      in there as a book-marker. That's all!*]

AFTER-THOUGHT.—The answer, though ungrammatical and prevaricatory, is the only one possible under the circumstances. I expect the author didn't care much one way or the other, but merely thanked the "proof" for a grand opportunity to sling ink at me.

A PHOTOGRAPH.

NOTE.—Another photo-poem. There is no doubt Daguerre has a great deal to answer for in this matter of amateur effusions apropos of photographs. This is another of the patent-adaptable form of poem—may be sent to any one and at any time. Specially recommended for young or disappointed bards.

WHY do you mock me, dear, with this—
    The face I ne'er may see again,
The lips I ne'er again may kiss—
    Why do you send me so much pain ?

I sit and watch the sweet lips part ;
    I almost see them smile for me :
        A pretty thought, and very acceptable—saves one a deal of personal
        trouble.
But in the picture there's no heart—
    I doubt if there's a heart in thee.
        A common reproach, psychologically insulting, and pathologically in-
        correct.

The little foot peeps underneath
    That frock I've seen my darling wear—
        The author had evidently been reading Sir Thomas Suckling :
          " Her feet beneath her petticoat
          Like little mice peeped in and out," *etc.*
Ah, Sweet, these memories are death ;
    Your loss is more than I can bear !

Come back to me, and be mine own,
    This sounds familiar.
    And all the world shall count as naught ;

"MES AMOURS."

Within my heart you reign alone,
The queen of me in every thought.
The two "telling" lines of the poem.

Come back to me ! I cry in vain ;
Come back to me ! in vain I pray :
Your photograph, in dumb disdain,
Reminds me you are far away.

AFTER-THOUGHT.—An incontrovertible poem, though obviously a mixture of truism and paradox. Strange that men can be so inconsistent as to live after writing such verses as these.

LET IT BE SOON.

LET it be soon !   Life was not made to long
  For far-off hours in dim futurity.
Thy presence soothes me like some distant song.
  Oh ! where my head has rested, let it lie.

> Pretty, and calculated to advance matters with a rush.   This seems to
> assume that the author is *au dernier bien ;* and when one expost-
> ulates he can shelter himself behind poetic license—in more senses
> than one—and the fevered imagination of the bard.

Hope is the morning, Love the afternoon.
                            Let it be soon !

Let it be soon !   The treasured daylight dies,
  And changes sadly to the chill of night ;
But summer reigns forever in thine eyes,
  And at thy touch grief stealeth out of sight.

> A potent argument, and warranted to kill if not too freely diffused.
> This was too freely diffused.

After these years of longing, let Love swoon.
                            Let it be soon !

AFTER-THOUGHT.—An ideal poem for "general" use. Should be copied in manifold, and carried continually for distribution at critical intervals ; but should be distributed to people who don't know one another, as it is the kind of poem that women always show one another—in confidence.

FROM MY FLY-LEAVES.

NOTE.—A well-known author of my acquaintance has been in the habit of sending me his books as they come out, with little verses dedicatory scribbled on their fly-leaves. I have singled out these two as being the most complimentary and pretty, and the answer to the first as being clever though rude.

FROM THE FLY-LEAF OF A BOOK THAT I "INTERRUPTED" BY MAKING HIS ACQUAINTANCE.

THE first part is dull—because then I knew not
The genius of life that you hold in each look ;
The last part is duller—to know you I'd got,
And, knowing you, how could I think of my book ?

[I lent the book to a juvenile bard who cherished the superstition that he had adored me, but that I was false and faithless—idiosyncra-cies, both of them. On seeing the above, he dipped his pen in gall and wrote the following.]

OH ! why should the thoughts of the false little Doll
Interfere with the course of constructing a vol. ?
Hawk preys not on hawk ; brother bothers not brother ;
Why should one piece of fiction embarrass another ?

AFTER-THOUGHT.—*Lovely !*

FROM THE FLY-LEAF OF A SUBSEQUENT WORK, AT THE " CON-
STRUCTION " OF WHICH I ASSISTED.

THOUGH critics may deride, dear,
  Though few the readers be ;
I wrote it by your side, dear,
  And that's enough for me.

——————

ANOTHER.

THE critics say the world's not so,
  And call me cynical and snarling ;
But then, one fact they did not know—
  I wrote it ere I knew thee, Darling.

AFTER-THOUGHT.—The great charm of snap-verses of this kind lies in the fact that the
bard has to come to the point at once. so cannot shelter himself behind the periphrastic ambig-
uousness which is, at once, the privilege and the protection of bards.

A QUESTION.

NOTE.—Another title recommended as patent, on account of its adaptability; it seems to be based on the advice of the philosophic luminary who said, "If you want to inculcate a fact of which you are yourself not quite certain, state it boldly, but interrogatively."

D——Y, has it ever crossed your thoughts
Leave blank for name, and alter to suit metre.
That we were made for one another ?
It certainly had not struck me in that light.
Had something else been otherwise,
Deliciously vague, this.
We might have lived and loved together ?
Possibly ? The " premises " are too vague to allow of definite reply.
'Tis said that in this world below
Each soul would find a sister-half,
If only they knew where to meet—
Surely, there are lots of places ?

.   .   .   .

But better never meet at all
Than thus to meet—and meeting, part !
Parfaitement !

.   .   .   .

Can it be true that you will never, dear,
Unbind that glossy hair for me ?
Can it be true I ne'er again shall press
Impassioned kisses on your lips ?
Or lay my cheek upon that polished arm ?
" Cheek " was a dangerous word to have used.
Can this be true, whilst knowing *what* I know ?
Classic uncertainty again.

I dream of you and watch your portrait's eyes,
In foolish hope that they will turn on me,
In silly craving they might smile on me.

.   .   .   .

The convict feels a lighter chain,
Who hopes for future liberty :
But I—my Darling, give *me* hope !
The awful commonplace of life
Must separate, for weeks, for months, for years :—
But tell, " Sweet Sister-half," that I have found ;
When next we meet, will you say, " *Never-more ?* "

I don't even know now, as we never met again.

AFTER-THOUGHT.—The tumultuous " Walt-Whitman-esqueness " of this " measured prose "
is not without its charm, but this, as a whole, is deprecatory with the wrong sort of deprecation.
Humility should always be arrogant (pardon the paradox !), otherwise it is apt to miss fire.   If
I remember rightly, this missed fire.

A DREAM-WISH.

NOTE.—And it *really* deserves to be fulfilled, for it is the least *exigeant* poem I have ever had hurled at me. One feels inclined to say, like the lady in the French play, whose lover announces his intention of going into the business of thinking only of her, to whom she replies, cordially, "*Faites-donc! Faites-donc!*"

I.

WHEN sleep rests on my eyelids, and the train
 Of fairy fancies from the realm of dreams
Comes with its wand to stir my drowsy brain,
 And wake my senses to the golden gleams
  Of joyous scenes that make my sleep more sweet,
  My happiness is made the more complete
If in my dreams I see thy face again.

   How easy it is to give pleasure to one's fellow-creatures if one would
   only take the trouble!

II.

I'd never wake if thou wouldst but abide
 In dreamland evermore, and lovingly
Wouldst nestle close and trusting at my side,
 And give thyself with all thy heart to me.
  For, waking, I might find thee cold and stern—
   Probably!
  A goddess, on whose altar I might burn
My heart to ashes, and gain naught beside.
   Ditto.

AFTER-THOUGHT.—This also is rather the lay of a lazy lover. I told him so, and he sent me a hundred verses, which, on the death of two compositors, I have finally decided not to print.

THE IMAGINING OF A FEVERED IMAGINATION.

NOTE.—The author of the following lines *might* just possiby have saved himself by their title, but he *didn't* risk it, *i.e.*, I never knew who wrote them, though I have compared the writing with hundreds of others ; and I give them as the most *piano* specimens of dozens like unto them— only worse—that I have received from unknown bards with equally convenient (for me and them) imaginations.

THEY praise the shape of thy form so fair,
> An inferior line ; but he hadn't yet settled down to his stride, I suppose.

Sweet Mistress, mine ;
Thy coral lips, thine auburn hair,
And eyes that shine !
But these charms thro' a dull, cold veil they see,
> By order of the Lord Chamberlain.

And that veil is lifted alone for me—
When the rich brown mass of thy glossy hair
[Its waves unbound],
Sheds o'er thy beauty a mantle rare,
Floating around,
Striving to hide, with envious skill,
Thy bosom soft and glowing,
White as the snow, without its chill,
> What an imagination !

While far beneath the wild veins thrill,
Like Hecla's lava flowing.
> *I* put in "*Hecla ;*" *he* said " *Hector*," but I don't think there's a volcano —or a moth—of that name.

Tis mine to divide each glossy tress,
From that soft and yielding form ;

'Tis mine alone to hear thy sigh
  At passion's height,
When flames, as if electric, fly,
Convulse the frame, illume the eye.

      Edisonian, to say the least of it. N.B.—This verse has been a good deal Bowdlerized.

Their hearts, their very souls, they'd give
For this short hour with thee :
  In this short hour with thee I live
      A whole Eternity.

      In imagination—as per title—*bien entendu !*

AFTER-THOUGHT.—And this is the kind of trash that is "metred" out (excuse me !) to any popular actress who appears—well—on the stage instead of in a box at the opera,—by the *yard.*

CARMEN

THE ANSWER.

NOTE.—This was sent me by a boy, who had, in a moment of agony, confessed to me some terrible passages in his early life. As I really cared a little for him, I was able to comfort him somewhat, and next day sent him the verses on page 6. This was his answer, written with the messenger-boy looking over his shoulder.

TELL me, dear Love, have you ever reflected
On how you have brightened this hard life of mine?
Tell me, my Sweet, if you ever expected
To make an existence so wretched, divine?

> Very complimentary, even if he didn't mean it.

Can you conceive how I lived ere I met you?

> Yes, perfectly.

Can you imagine a life without love?

> Well,—I don't know.

Dear, if you can, you know well why I've set you
All women who walk upon earth, far above.

> A very easy remark to make.

May you ne'er dream of the sickening sorrow
With which all my loveless "to-days" had been rife,
Till a wretched "to-day" turned a glorious "to-morrow,"
As your voice and your touch stirred my dead soul to life.

And this *you* have done for me, Dolly.   Ah, never
Forget that 'twas you broke the links of my chain,

> What a responsibility! and how dangerous! A woman never breaks
> a man's chain but she makes her own.

402636

And that all lies with you : shall I live thus forever ?
Or must I go back to the old life again ?

> As if you'd go if I sent you.

Come always to me in your thoughts, and remember
That here there beats always a heart that is true ;

> Oh ! man, man ! "Always," indeed !

And bid memory chaunt of that month of September,
When first you saw *me*, and at last I met *you*.

> Humility very delicately expressed. A most deadly line, implying, as
> it does, a life passed in endless struggles to this end. I can almost
> hear him sigh as he says "at last."

And, Sweetheart, if ever your courage should waver,
When I've gone away and the years onward roll,
Be strong for *my* sake ; for if you are o'ertaken,
I'm bound to fall too, since I've left you my Soul !

> This is the sort of verse most women would give their souls to believe.

AFTER-THOUGHT.—Really very pretty, and a very dangerous poem to receive. It appeals
to the maternal instinct, which, even if unexpressed, is so strong with "us." At the same time
there is in the above an apparent readiness to make the best of "anything" that is calculated
to find a weak spot in the barricade against the natural enemy, if such weak spot exist.

A LEGEND OF KING WILLIAM STREET.
MAY, 1879.

NOTE.—I hesitated about including these verses, as they are purely local; but their clever-ness and "Gilbertian" audacity of rhyme decide me to print them. It was at the Folly, in King William Street, Strand, that I played *La Perichole*, and first met the author of these lines.

THERE came from Pall-Mall a poor, desolate diner-out;
His clothes they were faultless, his manners superb;
From all the "Spring Captains" you'd ne'er pick a finer out.

"Spring Captains" are the young officers of the "Household troops," who promenade Pall-Mall during the season.

But sadly this ev'ning he steps o'er the kerb:
For William Street blazes no longer for Dolly,
With sweet music wedded to words of Tom Bowles;

T. B., editor of *Vanity Fair*, who wrote the English libretto of "La Perichole."

And dark seem the portals that lead to the "Folly,"
Where now maunders only old Sheridan Knowles.

"La Perichole," was followed by a revival of one of Sheridan Knowles' plays.

"Ah!" cries the fond youth, "while I lounged at the 'Gaiety,'
And gazed at the rhythmical legs of Kate Vaughan,

The queen of English step-dancers of this quarter-century.

And watched country curates contend with the laity
In clapping their Connie—so nice, though a raw'un—

The worship of "the child" Connie Gilchrist was then at its height.

I simply forgot that in all there's finality;
That even Sweet Farren's best antics may pall;

The "star" of the "Gaiety" burlesque company.

That only in Dolly lives constant vitality,
To quicken your pulse as you sit in your stall.

And now that vile Shepperton's swallowed my *Perichole*,
> I had taken a cottage to rest in at Shepperton-on-Thames.

And 'Women, dear Women,' no longer is heard,
The feeling that happiness all is at Jericho'll
    Make me do something or other absurd.
Oh, death ! I beseech, come take *this* wretch away, oh !
    I'll shoot or I'll hang me, now Dolly has flown,
Or else I will hie me to hunt Ketchewayo,
>   The South African imbroglio was then going on.

    Or sit through 'The Lady of Lyons'—alone !
No !   Into the river !   And then she'll be sure to see
    How I still mourn for those ev'nings so sweet ;
For old Father Thames, with his usual courtesy,
    Will bear my damp corpse to her miniature feet ! "

AFTER-THOUGHT.—A chapter of contemporary dramatic history, this. The experimental bard, if he knew the " consequences " of this poem, would take a lesson and write this kind of thing, instead of indulging in " the premeditated verbiage of irresponsible amorousness."

LONELY, BUT NOT ALONE.

NOTE.—This poem celebrates in verse (though retrospectively) the most charming epoch of an *affaire—i.e.*, the moment at which one has made up one's mind that one is quite content and wants nothing more ; the point at which nothing jars upon one, and the word "contentment" has not become, as it usually does, later on, a synonym for "carelessness."

THE silvery Thames was flowing past,
  There at our feet it hurried by,
And in delight too dear to last
      Prophecy after the event is a privilege of bards.
  We sat together—She and I ;
And if no words between us went,
It was that we were quite content.
      Vide La Fontaine, concerning the ostrich.

But one short month since fate, or chance,
  To where she was my steps had ta'en,
Since I had dared to break a lance
    With "someone else :"—had dared disdain,
And found, ere Doll an hour I knew,
A tender woman, sweet and true.

Oh ! happy days that followed then,
  When by the river-side we sat,
And talked of future glories, when
    The laurel wreath should spoil my hat ;
      He was a rising journalist at the time ; he has since risen.
And in that sky of Hope, serene
My gentle Dolly reigned as Queen.

All now is gone ; and I am here
  Alone, three thousand miles away,
To chronicle the social leer,
  To watch the social idiots play,
<small>He regulated the columns of a celebrated " society paper."</small>
While Yankee dandies draw the cork
To Dolly's health in far New York.
<small>His choicest anathema was always reserved for " the land of the brave, etc."</small>

Shall I despair, shall I let pass,
  The hopes on which alone I live ?
Consent to write me down an ass,
  No longer for that laurel strive.
Ah, no! I never *can* forget ;
With her I *will* be happy yet.
<small>This sounds familiar.</small>

I see her smile across the sea,
  I hear her voice within my soul ;
<small>If this sort of thing, apparently easy to bards, were to come into general use, the telephone and phonograph would be badly " out of it."</small>
Her clinging kisses come to me,
  Though leagues of sea between us roll ;
She sits beside me while I write,
And in my dreams we'll meet to-night.
<small>Excellent ! and most convenient.</small>

AFTER-THOUGHT.—Strange—is it not ?—that just as death produces inflation (physically and biographically), when one has parted from a bard, he never celebrates anything but the roses of life. Possibly the rose, being dry, is easily preserved, whilst the thorns, being fortunately brittle, break off or get absorbed by the blotting-paper of every-day existence.

RETROSPECTIVE.

NOTE.—This, again, is a grand adaptable title, like " After ; " and I strongly suspect that it is a patent-adaptable poem, suitable for sending round promiscuously to ladies who go to the theatre with, or are escorted home from balls by, bards. The rhythm, which may be described as "broken-tooth-comb metre," is strongly recommended to bards whose feelings are too strong for their scansion. Tumultuously pretty, nevertheless.

.   THERE
At the door she stood,
   So passing fair
   In the halo of her rich brown hair ;
        This line must alter to suit color of hair.
   What was it
   In her steadfast eyes
        Good universal description of eyes.
That reached the tear-well in my heart,
   Bade the drops rise,
And made it sad to part ?
        Goodness knows !

 .   .   .   .   .   .

   She did not love ;
She would not say she cared :
        What was the use after the preceding line ?
   And yet
Her look confessed regret,
   And had I dared
        Osez toujours !
To seize her in my arms
   And kiss her brow,

To break the spell her charms
  Had thrown around me ;
    And tell her how
I loved her—how she found me
  Sick of life and daily fret
  Till we had met ;

> I have heard this, *passim!* They all say this and we all like it, and believe it.

Had I kissed her soul away,—
  Till she were fain
    To say
Whether her heart were touched or nay,
  Though it were pain
  To part, it were not vain
  To hope that we might meet again.

> Seems almost a pity he did *not* dare. If I remember rightly, he didn't. One can't rely on the after-utterances of bards as statements of fact.

.   .   .   .   .   .

I see her there,
Like some fair statue stand,
  With streaming hair,

> This is unlikely.

And shoulders bare,

> This is not.

A living grace from some "antique."

.   .   .   .   .   .

And I can only kiss her hand,
  And once more
  Look into her eyes ;
    She will not speak ;
And now I close,
  With sighs,
    The door :

> They must have been powerful sighs.

And through the night
I watch her light
   Above,
  And mark
Her shadow as it comes and goes.

.   .   .   .

Alas ! the light is out,
  And all is dark :
Will she doubt
   My love ?

What else *can* she do, if the above is a reliable tabulation of the "premises" ?

AFTER-THOUGHT.—One feels inclined to quote Soyer or Francatelli, and say, in conclusion : "Flavour to taste, add coloring-matter and ornament, and serve hot on clean paper." A charming composition, however ; and as the writer is the author of several charming libretti, I recommend it to him for reproduction as a recitative. That is, if he hasn't already scattered it around too freely.

LES ACCROCHE-COEURS.

NOTE.—Written when it was the fashion to wear little curls at the outlying districts of one's hair, which we called *accroche-cœurs*.

WE neither said a word, and yet
  Heart spoke to heart, as side by side
     This garrulity of bards' hearts is most convenient.
     We stood that day—together :
No strangers, for we often met ;
  But still there seemed a gulf as wide
     As May and winter weather.
     He wants a word here.

I heard her breathing come and go :
     It can't have been me—I'm not asthmatic.
  My own heart beat so very fast,
     I thought it must be breaking.
Whether she cared for me or no
  I could not tell, but hoped at last
     Love in her soul was waking.

Her hand grew warmer, clasping mine,
     Not even a bard ought to tell his mistress that her hands are
     "clammy."
  And when our glances met, her eyes,
     I fancy, sparkled brighter ;
But Love as yet had shown no sign :
  I felt a tender, vague "surprise,"
     And clasped her hand yet tighter.

The perfume of her scented hair,
  The contact of her silken dress,
    Thrilled all my veins to bursting.
      Ça-y-est!
She *would* not speak—I did not *dare ;*
  For one love-draught, in sore distress,
    My anguished soul was thirsting.

And thus we stood, each other near,
  Without a word ; our eyes were bright,
    Than eyes of love far blinder ;
      I thought this idea was exploded in these days, when, as Tiffany says,
      "The price is legibly marked on every article."
And as I turned in dull, cold fear,
  Her profile came against the light—
    The window was behind her.

And there, beneath her looped-up hair,
  The little curls peeped out and smiled—
    And yet no word was spoken.
I could not help myself, but there
  I clasped her round, my darling Child ;
    Enfin !
And feeling now nor doubt nor fear,
I kissed her neck, and little ear ;

.   .   .   .

And as I pressed her finger-tips,
She turned and gave me up her lips—
    How shocking !
      And so the ice was broken.

AFTER-THOUGHT.—This poem should have been inspired by a return from a ball, when *He* is just saying good-by. If I were writing this scene for a play, I should describe it thus : A little low cottage in a quaint garden. Though the month is July, at this early hour the air is sweet and fresh. The garden-door, swinging to, shuts out the London street and life. Once through the porch and open door, they stand in the hall, in that deadly quiet 'twixt dying night and living day, and take the first step toward making each other happy or——miserable—most probably the latter. I wonder if the real inspiration was anything like this ?

RÉVERIE.

WITH all the chill of friendship in mine eyes,
> Yes, it is always there.

With all the fire of longing in my soul,
> Most satisfactorily hidden.

I lie alone—for you are gone—and watch
The cinders, busy in their idleness,
Writhe into wreaths and stumble into shapes,
To fall once more and leave no trace behind
Of the weird fancies of the dying fire :
> Charming ! I've used this myself somewhere else.

Its last confession—as it were—before
It crumbles into dry, decadent dust !

Who was the Sage who, in rough days of old,
> God knows. I don't know anything.

When flight of time was marked alone by lust
Of life and near approach of chillsome death,
Said that, of all things dangerous and bad,
The worst was when a woman thought alone ?
> I hear that this was Juvenal. Probably ! he was nothing if he wasn't rude to ladies.

He spoke in wanton ignorance that man,
Left solitary with his own drear thoughts,
Is worse a thousand-fold ; for he blasphemes
The world and all things, dreaming of his past.
> My own pocket Manfred.

To lie and listen to the dying voice
Of dying day, in the great city's din
Hushed incoherent 'neath the folds of night ;
To lie, amid the cushions and the silks
Of your divan, and wonder whether it
Would speak of things more strange, could it but speak,
    Curiosity.
Than all these memories, which start from naught,
    Thrown on the screen of thought in bold relief,
    Cast by the magic-lantern of the Soul.

Wild thoughts of Days that had not any Night,
    How sleepy I must have been ! This would mislead people as to my
    mode of existence.
Of tingling joy in Life that knew not Death,
Of hours of Pleasure where no thought of Pain
Crept in to make the pleasure dear to us ;
Of captive hours, chained in the bond of eyes
That shone on us alone, and bade us drown
Of such conceits as " Time " and " Space " the thoughts,
    When we lay drugged in lethargy of love,
    And fancied our unconsciousness was peace !

To lie, contrasting with our happy hours,
The wretched ones when those that we have loved
Seemed cold, or disappointment chilled the fire
    Too many chills, my friend—you'll get influenza.
Of longing in our hearts and bade despair,
Distrust, and disenchantment take its place ;
Of moments when our hearts have beaten high
With wild expectancy of joys supreme ;
    Of how those moments faded into dull,
    Cold misery, when Nothingness ensued.

Ah, well! why mock the solitary hours
With thoughts like these ?   Rise up, contemplate
The Present, with its dazzling brilliancy
That shines into our eyes and bids us cease
To think at all of Future things or Past !

Ah, there ! Omar Whayyam !

The " now " is good ; take heed lest you, by calm,
Dispassionate reflection, 'neath the rose,
    See the sharp thorn of Disillusionment,

Very sound philosophy—always avoid the thorns.

As through a murky lens th'astronomer
        Sees spots upon the sun !

[The following note was pinned to the poem.]

DEAREST DOLLY: Don't leave me alone with myself in a place where you have been ! I get upon my nerves and think of things that never have been, till my mind wanders away and leaves my body mad.   Yours,

AFTER-THOUGHT.—This boy was possessed by the original idea that he was not, never could be, jealous. Oh, Vanity, thy name is not always woman !

AFTER.

NOTE.—This should have been called "An Interlude." I think it is in the nature of the skeleton-key—adaptable to the dead-locks of flirtation. Poem suitable for sending to a loved one before going out of town, where one *may* find someone one likes better. Its great advantage is that if the above does not take place, one can triumphantly point to the last verse, and, working the "misunderstanding" racket, start fresh.

I FELT, long ago, that my day-dream was past ;
    But I know 'twould have softened the sting of my pain
Had you told me *yourself* that I'd wakened at last,
    Had I heard your sweet voice only once, once again.

> Introductory verse easily explained, if necessary, by referring to some casual tiff on some trivial subject.

'Twas your cold, cruel silence that taught me despair,
    When no word echoed mine as I whispered your name ;
Your answer, unspoken, was cruel to bear,
    And I left you in silence—ah ! was I to blame ?

> Clever, because completely unanswerable. Nothing to lay hold of, but effect all the same, viz., " he left me in silence "—explanation might have been too definitive.

And now it's all over : I know 'tis too late,
    And I know ere we meet that 'twill be but to part ;
But grant me one sign, for this pain 'twill abate
    If it come from *your* lips, from *your* hand, from *your* heart.

> A thoroughly jesuitical verse, suggestive of the gentleman who said " I go," and went not. Note the artful italics in the fourth line.

If only you'll tell me that thus you will be,
    Ever silent perhaps, yet in silence the same ;
If my soul turns in mute adoration to Thee,
    If I love you in silence—ah ! am I to blame ?

After writing this—go ! Don't wait to be told. The prevision of the second line saves a world of trouble.

AFTER-THOUGHT.—A most useful poem, and adaptable to nearly every stage of a *toquade.* It also has the supreme advantage that it may be sent even after the lapse of years, and in explanation of innumerable infidelities.

EROTIC CHESTNUTS.

NOTE.—This was written me just as this volume was going to press, by a friend who looked over some of the MSS., and to whom I remarked on the sameness of their expressions. He was touched at a sore point evidently, for he sat down and wrote me the following, under the above title.

You tell me all men say the same
  Mendacious things when they adore!
  They do.
If so, you ought to lay the blame
  On all these men who've loved before :
  There'd be plenty to go round.
For surely you've no right to scold
  Me when I say that " *Only you*
Have understood me "—if it's old,
  A male version of the *femme incomprise* fiction.
  It need not therefore be untrue !
  Not *necessarily.*
And when I say that " *I unbend*
  Alone for you, and show myself,
  This is almost—eh ? What ?
You need not cease to be my friend
  Because 'twas said by some poor elf
  It was.
Who doubtless *also* said what I
  Say now to you, that "*Any day*
I'd gladly lay me down and die
  If you should find me in your way ! "
  Vide AFTER-THOUGHT on p. 28.
And possibly e'en *you've* denied
  The truth of statements such as this :
  I have.

I'm only happy by your side! "
> This would be all right if one never saw them with anyone else.

And *" Loving you is simply bliss ! "*
> A veritable *marron glacé.*

'Tis possible these *have* been said
  By men flirtatious, bad, and bold,
> They have.

But, oh ! I *trust* you'll not be led
  To doubt them *now*—because they're old !

Envoy.

Now listen to me, and henceforward be wise :
  " I never have loved any woman but you "
Was remarked by *Père* Adam in Paradise,
  Since when—as a statement—it's been untrue !

AFTER-THOUGHT.—" None but the brave deserve the fair," and this man deserves *anything* —even immortalization as one of " Mes Amours," though a frivolous and irreverent one.

MY OWN.

A CONSOLATION.

NOTE.—Oh ! *why*, when my inmost soul yearns for the harmony of graceful, flowing rhythm, will my pen only jingle the monotone of rhyme? My spirit prays for Pegasus, and is confronted by the Rhyming dictionary: Heart, part, start, dart, tart, smart ; love, dove, glove ; stove, move, prove ; and so on. My rhymes remind me of the maddening musician mercilessly miscalled, who thinks, because with the forefinger of the right hand he can pick out a tune in the treble, "The claims of concomitant bass ! Have nothing to do with the case, Tra-la !" and so continues till, to the educated ear, agony reaches the end of the gamut in consecutive fifths and octaves, and desperation supervenes. Thus, for instance :—

DEATH and I walk side by side,
He the Bridegroom, I the bride ;
He whom I've so oft defied
Will no longer be denied ;
Whilst between us, yawning wide,
Lies a Gulf—a rushing tide
Of a Fear I dare not hide :
Dismal Fate, to be allied
To a Spectre who must guide
Evermore my every Stride.

[*Change of rhyme,—thank heaven !*]

Many in Health still share my Fate :
Soul bound to Soul, in Bonds of Hate ;
Life linked to Life, not Mate to Mate ;
Their Chaunt eternal, " Too late ! Too late !"

[*Once more ;—thank you !*]

I'd sooner my grisly Bridegroom keep,
   Than change with lives like this, all Strife ;
For I, too, have known what it is to weep,
   In my Soul, at the sound of the words " My wife."

AFTER-THOUGHT.—Why should an initial error trammel one within the sordid boundaries of similarity of metre ?   Bards, let us not be slaves !   Let us, like the ostrich, stop our ears to criticism, and do as seemeth, not best, but easiest to us !   Also N.B.:—Without the Capitals this Poem would be nowhere !

A WORD OF INTERPOLATED APOLOGY.

THE following two poems (pardon—rhymes!) were written after reading a volume entitled "Passionate Poems." I had fallen in love, and with me the divine disease of Eros lasts, as a rule—let us be accurate—about six hours and three-quarters; and being, as a natural consequence, full of fervid frenzy, it occurred to me that the sacred fire had entered into my breast (I believe that is the point it usually attacks). I was deliberate, as a poet should be, with my preparations. I thought that if I could mix up the words "Love," "Hell," "Desire," "Hate," "Soul," "God," "Love-drouth," and "Limbs"—all with capital letters [*vide* preceding specimen]— together with my own yearning agony, I, too, might make happy homes desolate and uncomfortable. In the throes of this particular passion, which lasted close on seven hours, I "threw off"—I believe that is the expression sacred to dogs and doggerel—the following, and sent them per messenger-boy to the Object in the early morning, hoping he had slept well, and that after his night's rest he would be strong enough to bear the shock. I am not altogether "satisfied with their manner," but "there's a deal of pleasure" in stringing them together.

MY QUESTION.

NOTE.—I forgot to say that this Object was the Oriental who always called me Māhmouré *Vide* p. 22.

I WONDER if when I am dead and cold,
My Spirit can visit this Earth again?
If so, I will come when the night is old,
And tap, and tap, at your window-pane.

I wonder if you will consider it odd
That Māhmouré's spirit should wander
So far from its home in the land of God,
Which is yonder, far distant yonder?

I wonder if you will expect me, dear,
In the soft gray chill of that early morn;
I wonder if you will reject me, dear,
And turn me away for some love new-born?

? ?

AFTER-THOUGHT.—The Object told me this was not up to my usual standard of idiotcy, but that I had cribbed it from " Violet Fane." I hadn't, I swear, but I felt so flattered that I wrote a lot more. If I have cribbed unconsciously, I trust that the beautiful poetess will forgive me, and feel gratified at receiving my drop of flattery to swell the ocean of adulation in which she floats in her everlasting youth.

HIS CONFESSOR.

NOTE.—This was written to re-assure a boy who had confessed to me some of the crimes of his fevered youth, and then was stricken with fear lest he should have hurt my feelings and driven me away.

Now, she said, let me confess you :
    Pour from your heart all its woe ;
Speak, and let no fear possess you—
    Half of your sorrow I know.
> Always a safe thing to say, and very encouraging to a juvenile adorer.

Come, place your head on my breast, love,
    Here, take my hand in your own ;
Tell me you feel more at rest, love—
    Tell me your sorrow has flown.
> The conceit of it is lovely, even to myself!

Silent ?   Why, what do you fear, love,
    That your story might drive me away ?
Not God himself—do you hear, love ?—
    Could take me, if you said "Stay!"
> This is a good breezy statement, calculated to kill on sight. If you announce the perpetration of an impossibility, let it be a good one, or the psychological effect is nowhere.

AFTER-THOUGHT.—The statement contained in the NOTE is not *la verité vraie*, but *la verité imaginaire*. The rhymes were written after reading a romance called, if I remember rightly, "The Suicide of Sylvester Gray," which impressed me a little at the time. Still, there was a lurking intention to convey an idea of the illimitable love which I might be capable of under proper treatment. *Vide* note on manufacture of chains, p. 37.

A FRAGMENT.

Do I wish we'd never met?
Do I wish I could forget?
As I ask, mine eyes grow wet
With a dew of sweet regret;
For *your* eyes are wondrous fine,
And they looked straight into mine,
With a gaze that was—divine
                [And deceptive].
And they said, "I love you well,
Better far than I can tell,
For your love my soul I'd sell!
            [You're *so* receptive.]
For you listen to my woes
As I sit here, at your toes,
Clad in such bewild'ring hose,
Till I think of *autre-choses;*
Then I sink upon my knees
By your side, by slow degrees,
And lay my head here—if you please?
           [I'm not expective.]

I will treasure every sigh
That you breathe when I am nigh,
And you know for them I'd die."
                 [I'm so collective.]
Still, the question *will* arise
[Very much to my surprise,
For I'm quoted, oh ! *so* wise
And *so* clever for my size],
Do I wish we'd never met ?
Do I wish I could forget ?
And my soul replies, " Not yet ;
                 Till we part
Let us yet enjoy the thrill
Of this pleasure—madd'ning still,
Let me give you all you will
                 Of my heart.
Let that heart to yours be near,
Let me stifle all my fear
Of that future time so drear,
When you've left me lonely, dear.
Don't remind me of the debt
I must pay, while you beget
Other loves—but oh ! *not yet*,
                 Not yet awhile !
For my heart with hunger cries,
Craves the food your hand denies—
.   .   .   .
Would you like a few more lies,
                 By the mile ? "

AFTER-THOUGHT.—This Fragment was my first offence, and was written the day after my " seven-hour passion " had announced his intention of striking camp and going " farther on." (I don't remember if he carried out his intention—I'll ask him.) Really that extra fifteen minutes has much to answer for. Oh, sympathy ! ! ! Oh, Plato ! ! ! you've more to answer for than Eros.

THE TRAGEDY.

NOTE.—I started out on this poem firmly believing myself to be befriended by the Tragic Muse. Alas! I was mistaken. I presume that I had some idea in my head when I started this lucubration—I will not do myself the injustice of believing otherwise—but that idea ingeniously evaded me at an early stage of the game. However, guessing, as a holiday pastime, is salubrious; maybe some good friend will guess for me.

HE came to my room in the dead of night,
  And all around was so still ;
My heart palpitáted in ghastly plight—
  I knew he would have his will.

I wondered at first was I certain quite,
  Did I dream, or was I ill,
When a full, soft ray of the moon's pale light
  Streamed over my window-sill ?

His terrible eyes had a look so bright
  That I feigned to lie asleep.
He murmured, rather than spoke, " I am right,
  I am right ! my vow I'll keep.
So you thought you could hide by taking flight
  Whilst I was out on the deep,
And you doubtless jeered at my wretched plight ;
  But now it's your turn to weep.
So it is for the man who betrayed me—
  As he sowed, so shall he reap ;
Very nearly his debt is repaid me,
  As close to your bed I creep."

He spoke very low, yet the words meant Death
  As plainly as tho' 'twere outcried ;
And nearer he crept, till I felt his breath
  On my cheek, then all hope died.

For I knew I had naught to say
That could purchase my Fate's delay ;
There was nothing to do but pray
That salvation might come my way.

Should I beg him his hand to stay ?
No ! I knew he would say me nay.
So in horror I trembling lay
'Neath those eyes of glittering gray.

He raised his hand, and the terrible steel
  Shone clear in the moon's pale beam ;
The plunge of the blade I began to feel,
  Then I uttered a piercing scream.

Again, again I shrieked, till waking,
I found a picture I held was breaking,
    And pieces of glass
    Were scattered, alas !
    All over the bed,
    From the foot to the head,
    And my fingers were red
    With the gore that was shed
    In that terrible fight,
    In the dead of the night,
With a ghost of my own home-making.
  5

Moral.

Gentle reader, take warning by me, and beware !
  Never take to your bed any dangerous toys,
  Such as pictures (for instance) of good-looking boys ;
Or, at least, if you *must*, take the glass from the frame,
Or you run a fair risk of just doing the same
As I did—and then have a bad nightmare.
  For, if you refrain from removing the glass,
  And lie on the picture, you'll find it disas-
Trous to nerves,—and have a bad nightmare.

Better still, if you'd flee from this mare of the night,
  I'd suggest circumspection *quâ* supper ;
Then read something light,
Effervescing and bright,
  Such as Browning, or Spencer, or Tupper.

AFTER-THOUGHT.—In confidence I will admit that, notwithstanding pretended humility in my inmost heart, I believed I had at last found the material for a great and serious epic. It is needless to say how soon I became conscious of my fatal infatuation. Luckily, when I reached the part where the gentleman should have done something tragic—and I could *not* think what to make him do, though I kept his hand up till he must have been quite exhausted—I suddenly remembered my Ingoldsby (bless him !) and rescued myself *à la* Fragment.

P. S.—Nothing but the despairing application of my publisher for more " copy " could have induced me to inflict this on my reader.

TO UNACTED AUTHORS.

NOVEMBER 28, 1887.

Having been fortunate enough to have sold my play "Fashion," to the lessees of Wallack's Theatre, it may be that a few remarks on the subject of launching a play will not be considered superfluous by those interested in dramatic authorship. If I am looked upon as lucky in having secured such a production for my first effort, let it not be supposed that the advantage was obtained without the expenditure of vast ingenuity.

Four years of weary disappointment formed the preliminary stage. Finally, broken down in health, nay, on the verge of the grave, I at last induced our much-respected manager, Mr. C——, to read my play. In the preceding two years he had got through two acts—an act a year. During the third year he read the third act, expressed much admiration, and desired me to send the remainder at once. I did, but Dramatophobia had set in, and no power could induce the poor gentleman to approach acts four and five. It was then, and not till then, that I brought to bear that merciless treatment which should never be resorted to but in extreme cases. There are a variety of means employed to obtain a hearing. A few hints from my own experience will not, I trust, be considered—to use the language of the XXXIX. articles—supererogatory. My remarks will be brief, if my words are long.

I do not propose to dissertate upon the many *un*successful means, but will dispose of them all by saying, "The club is no longer used." I place my method before the reader in the hope it may prove of service to those struggling genii whose efforts would doubtless conduce to fame but for the effete and turgid-minded manager. What England is to the oppressed Irish, what America is to that gentle, ill-used product of an alien soil—the Anarchist, so is the manager to the unacted dramatist !

My method, as shown in the annexed lines—with the accompanying newspaper-paragraph—is infallible, for the reason that, as in certain physical diseases, heroic treatment is necessary; so, I take it, the mental condition of the manager must be dealt with—no gentle measures, such as leaving MSS. at the door. The manager must be attacked when he is weak, helpless, alone. No quarter should be given to this despotic tyrant, who so frequently insists on managing his own business, and purchasing only that which to him seems best, to the detriment, if not the suppression, of the rising dramatist.

This desire on the part of the manager to use his own discretion should be met at the outset by the most virulent opposition. It is a base, sordid, pernicious abuse of power, which must not be tolerated, interfering, as it does, with the rights of the working author.

Therefore, I say, engage not with these vicious animals—managers—in kindly, courtly warfare, but strike boldly! strike, as I said before, not with the club, but with the more deadly, insidious poison, as prescribed, which has the advantage of killing on sight or obtaining a hearing. What I mean is that after all these years of unavailing effort, I sent him the following amazing production.

D. C.

NOTE.—The following verses brought to a triumphant *dénouement* the variegated diplomacy of *years*. They recount with the progressive detail of the English " Blue book," or " *Congressional Record*," the stages which led to the dramatic *coup d'etat* of last May. List, O ye who would bow before a curtain in response to the call for " Author."

SAID D—— to C——, my play you see,
  Upon the desk before you ;
Said C—— to D——, my misery
  Began the day I saw you.
> This, like most statements of fact, was uncivil, but incontrovertible.

        D. C. [Da Capo.]

Said D—— to C——, you'll soon be free,
  My work no more shall fret you ;
D—— take the woman ! said poor C——,
  I wish I'd never met you.
> He also said he'd have given a hundred dollars for me to have taken it to someone else.

        D. C. [Deuced Civil.]

Then C—— sat down, with lurid frown,
  Which melted to a smile ;
And as he read, resentment fled
  Before the siren's wile.
> After this, I took it away—*Il faut se faire valoir*. Alas ! it returned to him stronger by two acts.

        D. C. [Do Come to it.]

Poor C—— (they say), in blank dismay,
  Took up acts five and four ;
He said, I'd say, I hate this play,
  But I like it more and more.
    This was nice, if it *was* only said because I was a "picturesque ruin,"
    in the matter of health.
        D. C. [Distinctly Complimentary.]

Said C——, I'm gay! I've read your play,
  And very good I find it ;
The best I've seen for years I ween,
  And I guess there's cash behind it.
    Historians tell us that after this he went to a place called the "Hoff-
    man House" and "stood things."
        D. C. [Dollars Continually.]

To C——, D—— cried, I'm gratified,
  To think you're pleased, dear friend ;
And C—— replied, I'm satisfied
  Your trouble's at an end.
    This was on the principle, one for you and two for me.
        D. C. [Don't Congratulate yourself.]

In this MS. there's great success,
  Be patient as you've been ;
I trust bad health, with all this wealth,
  Will vanish from the scene.
    So did I.
        D. C. [Dolly Coincided.]

AFTER-THOUGHT [in doggerel this time].—

You're free you see, said D—— to C——,
  To try before you buy it ;

I will, said C——, if o'er the sea,
No English critics guy it.
A dying man clutches at a straw.
D. C. [Devilish Cautious.]

Moral.

The weasel cannot be caught asleep, says the natural historian, but I once heard of an animal of this kind that kept his eyes so wide open that he got dust thrown into them.

TRAGIC DEATH.

—

At four o'clock yesterday, the popular manager, Mr. C——, was found dead in his office. Assistance was summoned ; an autopsy was about to be held, when the Coroner discovered the above epic poem clasped in the dead man's hand. On examination, the Coroner said no further inquest was necessary. Death must have been instantaneous.

The jury added a rider to their verdict, expressing a hope that the Legislature would be shortly petitioned to take steps to protect defenceless managers and editors from the ravages of the rabid insect—whether indigenous or imported—known to science as *Scriblerii incipientes.*

POSTSCRIPT.

IF for a moment I madly believed
That *I* could write verse, my mind is relieved
      Of doubt on that score;
But of nonsense like this, if I only had time,
And hadn't to bow to th' exigence of rhyme,
      I could write volumes more.

        S. D.,
         Regretfully.

AU REVOIR.

WITHOUT wishing to render my apologies wearisome by repetition, I must, in justice to myself, make one last effort. Those who only know me through the medium of this little book could scarcely help thinking me heartless, cruel, and unable to appreciate the sentiment I have been happy enough to inspire. This is not so. No girl has treasured her first love-letter with greater tenderness than have I my verses. They have many a time consoled me for some fancied slight, or for one of the many disappointments of my profession. I am not ashamed to say I have loved them better than jewels (perhaps it is lucky for me I did). Those who know me will understand that, in making a joke of the verses sent me, I do so in no spirit of raillery, but because I cannot help laughing at the most serious subjects in life ; and it is because I believe many persons will sympathize and laugh with me—at least, I hope so—that I have made this little book.

SELINA DOLARO.